Pedro the Brave

by Leo Broadley

illustrated by Holly Swain

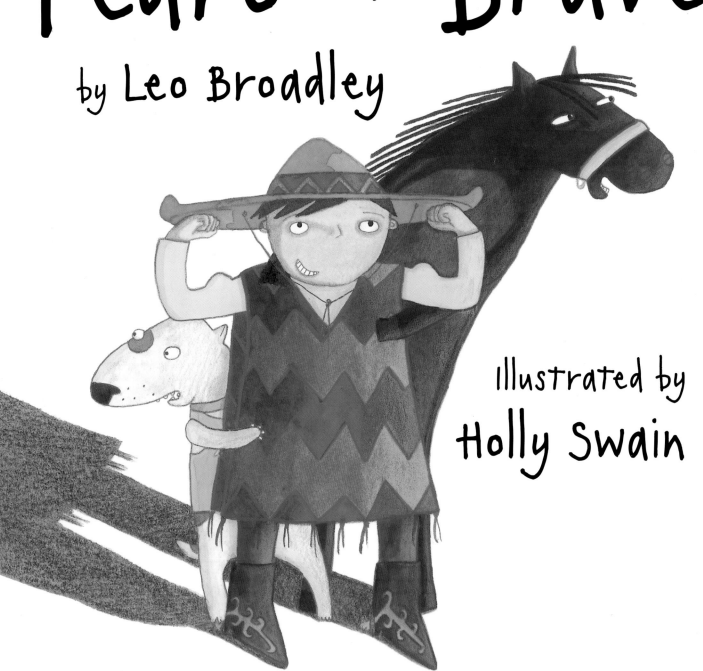

tiger tales

To Colin, Avril and Simon
who I love very much.
L.B.

To Daniel, Jasmine and Hannah.
May you all be as brave as Pedro.
H.S.

Sherriff

tiger tales
an imprint of ME Media, LLC
202 Old Ridgefield Road, Wilton, CT 06897
Published in the United States 2002
Originally published in Great Britain 2002
By Scholastic Children's Books, London
A division of Scholastic Ltd.
Text copyright © 2002 Leo Broadley
Illustrations copyright © 2002 Holly Swain
CIP Data is available
First U.S. hardcover edition ISBN 1-58925-024-9
First U.S. paperback edition ISBN 1-58925-375-2
Printed in Dubai, UAE
1 3 5 7 9 10 8 6 4 2

I'll tell you a story of Pedro the Brave
that will make all your whiskers go curly.
It's about using your wits to keep wolves
    from the door,
and why you should go to bed early.

It was one night in June, with a bright August moon,
under millions of twinkling stars,
that Pedro and Dusty and Ronnie the horse
were dancing and playing guitars.

ta da de daa
ta da de da

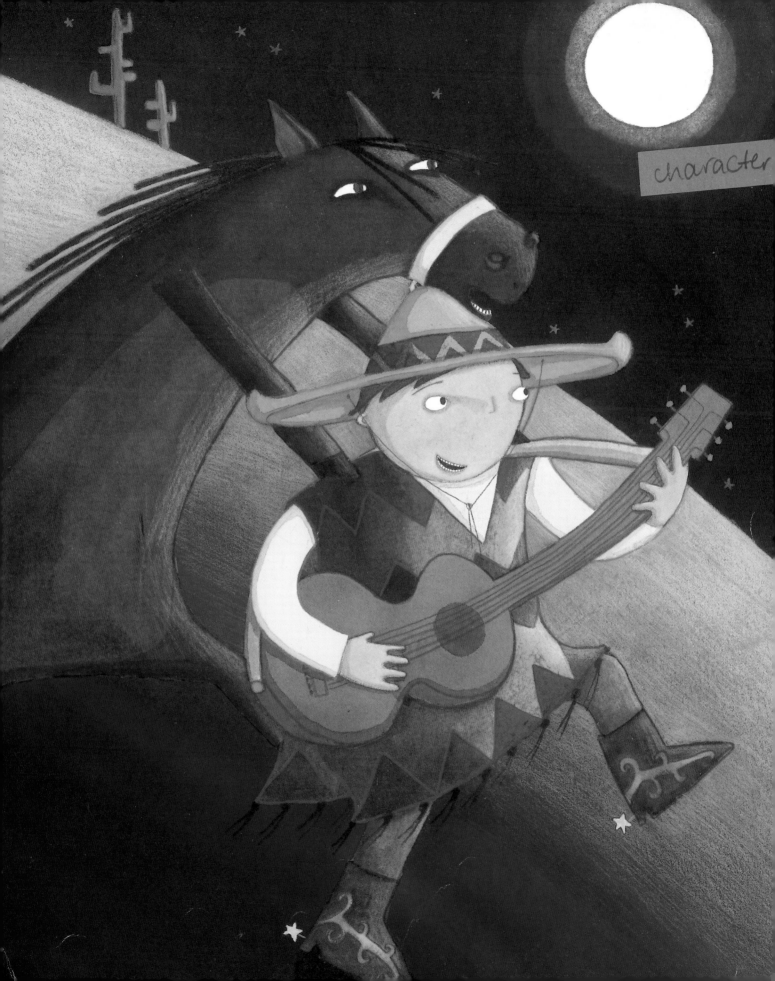

When there in the wood, a timber wolf stood,
with a tongue that was dripping and red.
He came to the fire and sat himself down.
"It's a fine night for singing," he said.

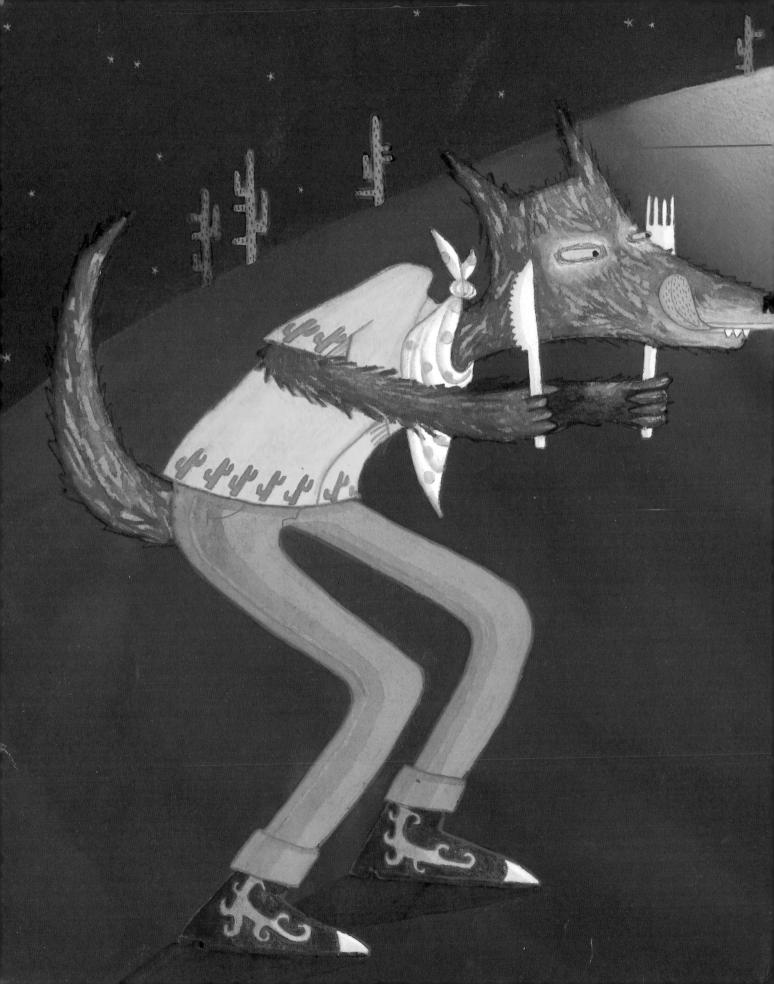

Now everyone knew that the wolf wanted meat,
and didn't know how to behave.
He wanted to gobble all three of them up—
it's a good thing that Pedro was brave.

"I have an idea!" Pedro said to his friends,
and he made up the stove nice and hot.
Then he turned to the wolf with a bow and he said,
"Would you kindly get
into the pot?"

"I'll make you a deal,"
said Pedro the Brave.
"If I'm going to be the first course,
I'll jump in this pan with no fuss at all,
if you'll just let me cook my own sauce."

"I need Tabasco and whiskey and dynamite dust, gunpowder, garlic, and ham. Cactus, paprika, and vindaloo paste, mustard, green chilies, and jam."

Pedro turned to the wolf and he said with a smile,
"Before I am part of your diet,
just put a drop of this sauce on the tip
   of your tongue—
I'm eager for someone to try it."

Now when I say it was hot, it really was hot!
It was hotter than flames on your toes.
It blew the wolf's socks off, his shirt and his pants,
it shot flames from the end of his nose.

"I feel ill," moaned the wolf,
"and my mouth is on fire,
there are bombs going off in my head.
I feel like I've eaten some firework pie—
I'll go and eat ice cream instead!"

Pedro the Brave put some wood on the fire.
"Now before we all go off to bed,
pick up your guitars under twinkling stars—
it's a fine night for singing,"
he said.